WHEN I HAD WINGS

SUSAN GATES

EGMONT

First published in Great Britain 2003
Egmont Books Limited
239 Kensington High Street
London W8 6SA.

Text copyright © Susan Gates 2003
Illustrations copyright © David Frankland 2003

The moral rights of the author and the illustrator have been
asserted

ISBN 1 4052 0609 8

1 3 5 7 9 10 8 6 4 2

A CIP catalogue record for this title
is available from the British Library

Typeset by Avon DataSet Ltd, Bidford on Avon

Printed and bound in Great Britain
by the CPI Group

CONTENTS

ILLUSTRATED BY
DAVID FRANKLAND

CHAPTER ONE

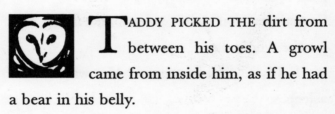ADDY PICKED THE dirt from between his toes. A growl came from inside him, as if he had a bear in his belly.

'Shut up, yer noisy creature,' Taddy told it. 'There ain't no more grub.' Not until suppertime anyway. He'd already eaten the bread and onion Ma gave him for dinner.

Taddy shivered. It was springtime, but the wind was chilly. It cut through his thin clothes. The pale-yellow sun was too weak and watery to warm him much.

A crow came swooping down into the field.

Taddy clacked his wooden rattle, made a half-hearted rush at it.

'*Yaaa*!'

The crow flapped lazily off. But it would be back, probably with all its friends, to guzzle up the farmer's seed. Taddy hated bird-scaring. He'd even rather chop the tops off turnips or pick up stones. Bird-scaring was lonely work. Sometimes, you didn't see another living soul for the whole day.

Taddy's eyelids sagged. He was almost asleep.

Something shrieked above him, a wild, harsh cry.

Taddy's eyes shot open. 'Hawk!'

The hawk was gliding high up on warm air currents. As if the wide blue sky were its personal playground. Taddy's eyes grew bright with longing. 'Wished I could do that.'

Hawks were his favourite. But all kinds of birds fascinated him. Swallows, seagulls, even crows.

It made his heart leap with longing, when he saw them flying. He wanted that kind of freedom for himself. To fly away, like they did, to faraway places.

He told himself stories about where they were going. He'd seen pictures in books at school before Ma stopped him going. She'd said, 'Now Pa's not working, you've got to be the man of the family. Bring some money in.'

Taddy imagined those hawks, swooping low over forests that stretched for miles. Where there were mysterious castles, and wolves roamed wild. He imagined the seagulls, skimming low over glassy green waves, as high as houses, with foamy tops. Where whales blew fountains and pirate ships searched for treasure islands.

His long, lonely days in the fields were full of dreams of escape and adventure.

Taddy sighed. He knew he was just tormenting himself. I'll probably be crow-scaring for the rest of me life, he thought.

He stopped telling himself stories. Found a little twig. Used it to rake in his ear for cockroaches. Ma said they sometimes crawled in there while you were asleep, ate your brains.

'Hey there!'

Taddy's stomach gave a sick lurch. It was the old devil. His Master, the farmer, was always sneaking up on his workers. He liked to surprise them – catch them slacking. Then he would start his roaring.

'You good for nothing! What do you think I'm paying you three shillings a week for?'

Then he would get out his horsewhip. That whip cut something cruel. Taddy still had the scars on his back from the last time the old devil had caught him. Master never tried to beat William who was thirteen, only two years older than Taddy. But that's because Taddy was a skinny little scrap and William was a young giant who could tuck a sheep under each arm and stride across fields with them. And William was a good worker. He didn't spend his days longing for escape, telling himself stories, like Taddy did.

Panic-stricken, Taddy sprang to his feet. Where was Master hiding? Any second now, his scowling face, with its bird's-nest beard and big strawberry nose would pop up, over the hedge.

'I caught you, you young varmint!' he'd cry. 'Daydreaming again! I'll tan your hide!'

'*Yaa*! *Yaa*!' Taddy whirled his rattle around his head, tried to look as if he was the best and busiest bird-scarer in the world.

A big white hat appeared over the hedge.

Eh? thought Taddy, confused. Master always wore a battered old straw hat.

A figure stepped into the gateway. Taddy forgot to clack his rattle. It hung useless by his side. His mouth dropped open. He gawped.

'Say, young feller,' drawled the stranger. 'There such a thing as a barn hereabouts?'

What's he saying? thought Taddy. He talks really peculiar! You could tell he didn't come from round here.

'A barn?' repeated the stranger, patiently. 'Hereabouts?'

This time Taddy understood. But he didn't answer. He just stared, his eyes wide as dinner plates.

The stranger was tall. He was dressed in dazzling clothes, white as an angel's. His jacket and trousers had fringes. So did his soft, white buckskin gloves. His belt had a gleaming silver buckle. He had a curly white moustache and long, white hair flowing over his shoulders. And the bluest blue eyes Taddy had ever seen.

The stranger stared back at Taddy. He saw a shivering little urchin, dressed in ragged clothes. His feet were bare. The stranger noticed that, under the dirt, they were blue with cold.

'Colonel Powhatten,' said the stranger. 'At your service.' He leaned over the gate and stuck out his hand.

Taddy didn't shake it. Instead he shrank back, like a startled hare. He looked ready to bolt at any second.

Darn, thought the Colonel. He'd finally found someone to ask the way. And it turned out to be the village idiot.

But he tried again. 'Say, you seem like a pretty smart boy. I'm renting a barn round here. From, what's his name now?' The Colonel searched his memory. 'From a Mr Hoggitt?'

That was the old devil's name. The sound of it made Taddy shudder. It loosened his tongue.

'Over there,' he stuttered, still staring and pointing a shaking finger.

'Thank you kindly, son,' said the stranger. He touched the brim of his white hat.

His blue eyes were friendly. And no one had ever, in his whole life, been so polite to

Taddy before. No one had ever called him smart. But the stranger had already gone.

Taddy raced over to the gate and climbed up it.

He saw the Colonel spring up lightly on to his white horse, flick the reins and go trotting down the muddy farm track.

Taddy clung to the gate, still staring. The Colonel had the fanciest riding boots he'd ever seen, all stitched, with silver spurs.

But even if he'd dared shout out, 'Hey, Mister, where did you get them boots?' the Colonel was too far away to hear.

Trundling after him down the track was a farm cart, pulled by two heavy horses. Whatever was inside, it was covered by a sheet of canvas.

Bird-scaring went right out of Taddy's head. He hared round the field to the other side. Panting, he pushed his way through a gap in the hedge. Spiky branches scratched him, but he didn't care. He wanted to get a good view. He wanted to spy on the stranger, see what he was up to. Taddy crouched down, his tatty head poking up above the tall grass.

The old barn was at the bottom of the hill. It was empty, apart from some rusty farm machinery. Taddy watched the stranger, sitting tall and splendid on his prancing white horse, with the farm cart lumbering way behind. At last it caught up with him, as he waited outside the barn.

The driver started to unload.

What's them things for? thought Taddy, spying from his hiding place.

Lots and lots of long poles. Big rolls of silky stuff. Taddy scrunched his face up in confusion. What was going on? He wriggled through the grass, a little closer.

'*Aaaargh*!' yelled Taddy. The Colonel heard his scream – turned to look.

Taddy felt himself grabbed by his collar, yanked back through the hedge into Hill Top field. He fell sprawling into the dirt. His nose was almost touching a big, clodhopping shoe, crusty with cow muck.

'Master!'

His heart pounding, Taddy looked up. He saw an angry, fiery red face.

'You young beggar!' roared the farmer. The crows clattered away in a black cloud. 'Look at them crows, getting fat on my seed, while you laze about. Did you think you could hide from me? You're for it now!'

The farmer raised his horsewhip, was about to bring it slashing down.

'No, Mr Hoggitt, no!' shrieked Taddy. He rolled himself up, hedgehog tight, into a ball. Wrapped his arms round his head.

He was already shivering, expecting the first blow. But it never came.

A white horse came soaring over the hedge. Landed light as a bird in the field.

Mr Hoggitt looked up, astonished. The

whip fell out of his hand. The horse reared high above him, chopping the air with its hooves.

'Who the devil are you?' he demanded.

The horse's rider swept off his hat. He made a graceful bow from the saddle.

'Colonel Powhatten,' he said. 'Stunt rider and sharpshooter. Star of *Buffalo Bill's Wild West Show*. Cheapest seats one penny, currently playing to sell-out audiences in London. At your service, sir.'

CHAPTER TWO

'Y OU WEREN'T BY any chance going to whip that young boy, were you, Mr Hoggitt?' asked the Colonel.

His voice sounded pleasant, easy-going. But his blue eyes, which had been friendly before, were hard as flint.

Confused, the farmer took a step away from Taddy.

'*Errr*, no.' He laughed, nervously. 'Course I weren't!'

He picked up a dazed Taddy, dusted him down. 'I wouldn't beat this young lad here. He's gem among lads he is, a jewel.'

'In that case,' said Colonel Powhatten, 'he's just the kind of youngster I'm looking for. Might I borrow him for a while? I've got work for him to do.'

'Borrow him?' grumbled the farmer. 'That'll leave me short of farm hands.'

'I'll pay you ten times his wages,' said the Colonel.

'I suppose I could do without him,' said the farmer.

'Mighty obliged,' said the Colonel, tipping his hat.

'Fine lad,' said the farmer, ruffling Taddy's hair. Taddy cringed.

Taddy watched the farmer stomp away. He still hadn't taken in what had happened.

'You're working for me now, son,' said Colonel Powhatten. 'Not for that shameless old bully.' The Colonel's eyes clouded over for a second, as if he was recalling something from his own past. Then he seemed to shake off his memories.

'Care for a ride on Starlight?' said the Colonel, as charming as ever.

Taddy felt himself hoisted up on to the horse. He rode in front of Colonel Powhatten, clinging on to Starlight's mane. He almost pinched himself.

'This is me, Taddy, riding with a star from Buffalo Bill's show!'

Buffalo Bill's Wild West Show was famous. Even in his tiny village they'd heard about it. It had brave cowboy heroes and black-hearted villains and shoot-outs and chases on real horses! Someone Ma knew had a cousin who had a friend who'd been to see it. She said, 'I fainted clean away twice, it were that exciting!'

And he wants me to work for him! thought Taddy, thrilled.

But even more amazing than that, the Colonel had stood up for him, saved him from a whipping. For that, Taddy would be his willing slave. Follow him to the ends of the Earth.

He scared the pants off Master, thought Taddy, chuckling. That old devil! He won't dare touch me now!

'What's your name, son?' asked the Colonel.

Taddy's answer came in a gush of words. 'Taddy short for Tadpole 'cos I'm small for my age but that ain't my real name –'

'Taddy will suit me fine,' said the Colonel. 'Well, Taddy, you and me, we've got a heap of work to do before sundown.'

The Colonel trotted Starlight straight into the barn. It was cool and dim inside. Doves looked down at them from the rafters and cooed.

This is better than freezing me toes off out in the field, thought Taddy. This is my lucky day.

He wasn't used to good things happening.

He wanted to tell the Colonel how grateful he was. But he didn't dare.

Instead, he decided to work his heart out.

First, the Colonel unfolded a big paper plan, spread it out on the ground. He studied it. Then took his jacket and hat off, rolled up his shirt sleeves. He picked up one of the bamboo poles. Taddy wondered, What's he mean to do with that?

But all the Colonel said was, 'Here, hold this steady. I need to saw it, just about here. See where I've marked it? Jump to it.'

Taddy jumped.

They sawed bamboo poles into different lengths. They glued them together. They bound the joints with twine to make them extra strong. Every few minutes the Colonel consulted the plan.

His fringed trousers and fancy riding boots were thick with sawdust. He stopped to wipe his sweating forehead, '*Phew*, hard work, boy.' Taddy copied him, '*Phew*!'

'Want some ginger beer?' said the Colonel, flipping the stopper out a bottle.

Ginger beer? Today was getting better and better. The Colonel swigged some, then handed it to Taddy. Taddy took a casual glug, just like the Colonel and pretended he drank ginger beer every day of his life.

They stood back to see what they'd made. The Colonel nodded with satisfaction. 'It's coming along fine.' Taddy nodded, as if he was pleased too. But privately, he thought, What the blazes is it?

It looked like a long, skinny ladder, made of bamboo poles. But it couldn't be a ladder. It was too light and flimsy to bear much weight. If that fat old farmer tried to climb it, it would snap like rhubarb sticks.

This time Taddy dared to speak.

'What is it?' he asked. 'That thing we been making?'

The Colonel looked amused. He put his finger to his lips. '*Shhhh*. All in good time, son,' he said. 'I'll tell the world when I'm good and ready. 'Til then, the fewer folk who know, the better.'

Taddy nodded again. So it was a big secret then? That made it even more exciting.

'Time for a bite to eat,' said the Colonel. 'Let's eat outside, under the stars.'

'*Stars*?' Then Taddy realised. The light coming through the barn door was different. It was silvery – from the moon not the sun. Day had changed into night and he hadn't even noticed. Suddenly, he felt as hungry as a wolf.

'Wait a second though,' said the Colonel, slapping his forehead. 'How could I be so stupid? I bet your ma'll be worried about you. You'd better hurry on home.'

Taddy shrugged. He didn't like to say so – but his ma probably wouldn't even miss him. Not with his brothers and sister squabbling and pestering her life out every second.

'Your pa'll probably be out hunting for you right now.'

'No, he won't,' said Taddy, shaking his head. 'My pa hurt his foot on the farm. It won't heal up. He just sits around all day on his backside, the great, useless lump,' added Taddy, quoting his ma.

'I 'spect he's a hard-working man, when he ain't sick,' said the Colonel, mildly. 'Cares for his family.'

Taddy was taken by surprise. He wasn't used to hearing nice things about Pa. Whenever Ma spoke about him there was scorn in her voice.

'Grab me some dry sticks then, boy,' said the Colonel.

Taddy searched around the barn. '*What's that?*' Something ghostly drifted by him, skimming low over the ground.

He smiled in relief. It was just a barn owl out hunting. Silent, no wing beats. Mice never heard them coming. Their broad wings let them float, like a kite.

They can fly as far as the moon. It looked like it sometimes, when you saw a big silver moon, with a dark owl shape swooping across it.

Half an hour later, Taddy stared into the red heart of the camp fire the Colonel had made. He felt happy. There were potatoes roasting in the hot ashes. His mouth was watering already. He wouldn't have to fight for his share like he did at home. At home, he had to fight for everything.

The Colonel was sprawled on the grass, his long legs out towards the fire. He took his clay pipe out of his mouth.

'This reminds me of when I was on cattle drives back in the old Wild West. That's in America, son, where I come from. I weren't much older than you –'

'America?' Taddy had heard of America, but he had no idea where it was. He'd never been further than the nearest village. He'd only been to school long enough to learn to write his own name – and gaze at pictures in storybooks.

'Me and the other cowboys,' continued the Colonel, 'we camped out many a night. We sure had some adventures –'

'What adventures?' asked Taddy. He loved hearing other people's stories. It made a change from having to make up his own.

'Oh, the time a grizzly bear come into the camp. And all the others, they run off –'

'A bear?' echoed Taddy, enchanted.

'He was a mean old critter,' said the Colonel, laughing. 'Bent on killing himself a man. He was seven feet tall –'

'Seven feet!' gasped Taddy. 'What did you do?'

'I sure wasn't going to fight him! And I couldn't reach my rifle. So I played dead. I can still feel his breath, burning my neck. He raked me with his claws. See here –'

The Colonel lifted up his long, white hair. Taddy saw a scar on his neck.

'The bear made that?'

'He sure did. Then there was the time we got attacked by timber wolves. And the time we was chased by a Sioux war party. I was saying my prayers then! Those Sioux braves,' said the Colonel, 'they sure were something to see – feathers, warpaint and all. They could shoot from the saddle. Get you right in the eye with an arrow while they was riding full pelt –'

Taddy juggled with his roasted potato. It was too hot, it burned his hands. But he didn't mind that. Now the Colonel was telling him how he'd swum a raging torrent in the old Wild West to rescue a drowning woman. 'Snakes alive!' said the Colonel. 'We was almost both swept over a waterfall!'

'If I'd read all these stories in a book,' cried Taddy. 'I wun't have believed them!'

Suddenly, the Colonel got up, kicked out the camp fire. Taddy stared at him, dismayed.

'I – I can't read anyhow,' he mumbled,

thinking he must have said something wrong.

But it seemed that the Colonel had just got tired of telling stories.

'You'd better get along home now, boy,' he said. 'I've got me a bed at the inn in the village. That's where I'm sleeping tonight.' Then he added, 'I'll see you tomorrow though. Here. At sun up.'

Taddy gazed after him, as he trotted off on Starlight. He sat so tall and straight in the saddle. The moonlight gave his white clothes a magical silvery sheen. Then he vanished and all Taddy saw was darkness.

There'd been a firework display once in his village. When it was over, when the last sparkling star from the last rocket had fizzled out, Taddy had felt strangely sad. He felt like that now.

He comforted himself, 'You're seeing him again in the morning.'

Tomorrow he might even find out what the

bamboo ladder was for. It was bound to be something exciting. What else could you expect from someone as dashing and brave as the Colonel, who'd spent his whole life having adventures?

Taddy trudged home, along the boggy farm track. The night was turning chilly. It was drizzling with rain. The kind of rain that made you cold right through to your bones. But Taddy didn't even notice. His mind swarmed with timber wolves, grizzly bears, fierce Sioux warriors and ladies rescued in the nick of time from swirling torrents.

Today you met a real, live hero. Taddy hugged himself with delight.

He'd often dreamed that his life would be different. And now it was.

Wait 'til I get home. And tell Meg what's happened.

CHAPTER THREE

T HE COTTAGE WINDOWS were dark. Everyone's in bed! thought Taddy. He hadn't realised it was so late.

He lifted the latch, stumbled inside into the pitch dark. There wasn't even the soft, yellow glow of a candle flame.

There was only one room in the cottage. Ma and Pa were asleep behind their curtain. He could hear Pa snoring. His three little brothers were in one bed, wriggling and whimpering like a nest of puppies. But someone was still awake.

His big sister Meg was crouched by the fire. She was warming her toes in the ashes, staring into the last glowing embers.

'Budge up,' whispered Taddy. He sat down beside her.

'*Eugh*!' A toad flopped over his feet. It lived in the cottage's damp corners. Sometimes, Ma swept him out with her broom: 'Get out you dirty creature!' But Pa was kinder. He said, 'Let him stay. He eats the cockroaches.'

'Meg!' hissed Taddy. 'Guess what happened to me today? I bet you can't!'

'Huh!' said Meg. She was in no mood to listen to one of Taddy's stories. 'Can't be no worse than my day,' she said.

Taddy's sister worked up at the Big House as a kitchen maid for Lady Violet. Meg was only thirteen, but she had a pinched old woman's face, white as mushrooms. And bags under her eyes like black stains.

'That Cook,' she whispered, before Taddy could get a word in. 'She's a witch! And she's got a wicked tongue. She calls me a thieving brat. She says, "You took some sugar!"'

'Did you?' asked Taddy.

'Only a little bit. Only 'cos I was hungry! Then she makes me polish the jelly moulds and scrub all the floors. Always ordering me about!'

Meg scowled, looked down at her hands. They were red raw from scrubbing. The skin was cracked open.

'That Cook,' she muttered. 'The way she puts on airs. All la-de-da! Thinks she's a lady.'

Taddy frowned impatiently. He was bursting to tell Meg his own news.

'Meg, I ain't working for Master no more. I'm working for Colonel Powhatten. He's from America. He's a sharpshooter and stunt rider and he's got a horse called Starlight and –'

'Oh, *him*!' Meg interrupted. She didn't seem impressed. 'I heard Cook talking about him.'

'Cook? What did she say?'

'I weren't really listening,' said Meg, nursing her sore hands.

A snappy voice came from behind the curtain. It was Ma. 'What's that row out there? Get yourselves to bed!'

Taddy crawled into the bed he shared with his brothers. They moaned in their sleep. 'Ow!' One kicked him. Taddy kicked him back.

Taddy squeezed himself into a little space near the wall. He couldn't sleep. His brain was buzzing with everything that had happened. The cottage was full of snores and the deep, steady breaths of sleeping people. He was the only one left awake. It was stuffy. The brother next to him suddenly made a big stink.

'*Phew!*' said Taddy, holding his nose. He

made his own personal breathing hole. He poked a finger through the wall right next to his head. It was easy to do – the wall was only made of mud and sticks. He sniffed in the clean, night air. 'That's better'.

Slowly, slowly, he fell asleep and dreamed of grizzly bears and wolves and Sioux warriors.

It was still dark when Taddy crawled out of bed, over his sleeping brothers.

Ma hadn't even lit the fire yet. She came shuffling out from behind the curtain, rubbing her bleary eyes.

'Taddy! Where was you last night? And what you doing up so early?'

Usually, she had to haul him out of bed with cuffs round the ear and threats. 'If you're late, that farmer will horsewhip you!'

'I'm off to work!' said Taddy, eagerly. He dragged his thin jacket on, shivering. Then tore off a hunk of bread from the loaf on the table.

'Put some of that back,' ordered Ma. 'Yours isn't the only belly needs filling'.

Taddy did. Ma was only tiny, but she was tough and fiery. She was handy with her hands too. If you made her lose her temper, better run and hide!

Outside everything looked grey and misty. But there were pink streaks in the sky – soon the sun would break through.

Taddy heard chittering from high above him. He looked up. Swifts! They darted about, quick as butterflies, on long, slender wings. It tugged at Taddy's heart, watching birds fly: *Wished I could do that.*

Swifts never landed on the ground, not once in their lives. Because if they did, they couldn't take off again. Pa had told him that. Imagine it, thought Taddy staring upwards, his head flung back, his mouth wide open.

Spending your whole life high up looking down on people. On crow-scarers like him, trapped in muddy fields seven days a week from dawn to dusk.

Walking backwards, still sky-gazing, Taddy bumped into someone.

'William! Where you off to?'

William gave Taddy a big sloppy grin. He had muscles like a strong man. But he wouldn't hurt a fly. People said he was simple, weak in the head. Sometimes, they made fun of him.

'I'm scaring them varmints today. Master says, "Not a one of them is to land!"'

'What, the crows?'

'*Yerp*,' said William. 'See, Master give me this'.

William clacked the wooden bird-scarer round his head. 'It makes a row!' he said, happily.

The swifts scattered, like shot from a gun. William stared after them, grinning. 'You're going to fly away like them, ain't you, Taddy? One day?'

William was the only one Taddy shared his flying dreams with, when they worked together sometimes, stone picking, or potato digging. He didn't even tell them to Meg. She would have laughed at him.

But today, Taddy didn't have time for daydreams. He had appointments to keep.

'I got to go now, William. I'm meeting the Colonel!'

Taddy hurried off in one direction, while William plodded in another, trying out his rattle on the way.

Taddy raced down the farm track, his bare feet splashing in the puddles. No one had been this way. Spiders webs, sparkling with dew, stretched across the path, from hedge to hedge. He broke through them as he ran.

Panting, Taddy hauled open the heavy barn door. Rushed inside.

He was too early. The Colonel wasn't here yet.

'*Phew.*' Taddy slumped down on the floor to get his breath back.

It was very quiet and still in the barn – like being in a church. Even the doves were still asleep. The first rays of sunshine came rippling in though the open door. Lit up that strange bamboo contraption they'd built yesterday. The plans weren't here. The Colonel had rolled them up, stuffed them inside his pocket.

'Don't want my rivals getting a peek at these,' he'd told Taddy, with a wink.

What's it for? thought Taddy, for the hundredth time. Perhaps today, the Colonel would tell him.

He wasn't sure whether he should be in here, without the Colonel. So he trudged outside to wait.

His belly felt hollow. Like a dog, he tore at his hunk of bread.

Then he heard hooves. He saw Starlight through the mist, looking like a ghost horse, a white rider on her back.

'Colonel Powhatten!' shouted Taddy waving, his mouth full of half-chewed bread.

The Colonel didn't sweep off his white hat and make a bow.

Instead, he leapt straight down from his horse. 'We got trouble, boy,' he said, leading Starlight inside the barn.

His friendly eyes were grim. His voice, so slow and drawling before, sounded urgent.

He seemed to forget that Taddy was a farmboy who knew almost nothing about the world. He spoke to him as if they were equals.

'I got back last night,' he said. 'And there's a telegram waiting. Says: *Arriving tomorrow. With photographer.* That's a whole week early!'

Taddy scrunched up his face. He was trying hard to understand what the Colonel told him. But he couldn't make any sense of it.

'Who's arriving tomorrow?'

The Colonel slapped himself on the forehead. 'Snakes alive! I forgot – you ain't got no idea what's going on.'

He crouched down, so his piercing blue eyes were on a level with Taddy's own.

'Look kid, I mean to make me a flying machine that will stay in the air for one whole minute. There's a competition, see, for the first one to do it. And I aim to win it! I just have to do it faster than I thought. You with me, partner?'

Partner! Taddy's heart swelled with pride.

'You can count on me!' said Taddy, nodding his head as if he wanted to shake it clean off.

Then, suddenly, his mind took in what the Colonel had just said.

'A – a flying machine?' he stuttered.

'Sure thing, boy,' said the Colonel.

'What, to fly like a bird?'

If anyone else had told him, 'I'm building a flying machine,' Taddy would have hooted with laughter. 'That's a good joke!' But the Colonel had swum raging torrents, escaped from Sioux warriors. If anyone could fly, he could.

'I've always wanted to do that,' stuttered Taddy. 'Fly like a hawk!'

But the Colonel wasn't listening. 'There's money in it too,' he was telling Taddy. 'Five hundred pounds prize for whoever does it first.'

'Five hundred pounds!' gasped Taddy. It was a fortune! If he'd had five pence he would have thought, 'I'm rich'.

The Colonel was already stripping off his jacket, rolling up his shirt sleeves.

'These fellers from London. They're coming tomorrow to time the flight, take pictures. Maybe they think I won't be ready! Well, by thunder, today you and me'll put this machine together and make her fly. See these plans?'

The Colonel unrolled the plans, put a stone at each end to keep them flat.

Taddy stared at them. At first they were just a jumble of lines. Then the Colonel began to trace them with his finger.

'We made one wing, see. We just have to cover it with silk. Now we make this other wing, and fix one above the other –'

Suddenly it all started to make sense. 'I see it!' cried Taddy excitedly. 'Like two big kites!' He'd made kites himself when he was small, from sticks and scraps of material.

'That's just it, boy,' said the Colonel. 'Only thing is, my machine doesn't have a name. When we win that prize, everyone's going to be talking about her. So she has to have a name. One folks'll remember.'

Taddy screwed up his face, thought hard.

'Hawk,' he said suddenly. 'Call her Hawk.'

'That's real good!' said the Colonel. 'I can see it now – on every front page from here to

Timbuctoo.' He sketched out a headline in the air. "COLONEL POWHATTEN AND HIS FLYING MACHINE, HAWK. THEY CONQUERED THE SKIES!" We'll be famous!'

'But ain't you famous already?' asked Taddy. Surely a man like the Colonel – hero, sharpshooter and stunt rider – was the most famous fellow in the world?

The Colonel coughed, '*Harumph!*' Did he look a mite embarrassed? But it didn't last, not more than two seconds. 'Come on, boy. Let's get busy!' he cried in a booming voice that echoed round the barn.

They sawed bamboo poles, stretched material tight over the wings, tacked and glued it into place. The glue stank like rotting fish. Sawdust clouds made them cough. Taddy was sweating and thirsty, but still they didn't stop. Hawk was being born before their eyes. Even though they were building her, it still seemed like magic.

'She's beautiful,' breathed Taddy, standing back to look.

'She sure is,' said the Colonel. He seemed as amazed as Taddy, as if he'd made a new discovery.

She almost filled the barn. She had two long, slender wings, one mounted above the other. Gauzy silk stretched over them. They glittered like a dragonfly. She had a tail behind her, shaped like a giant fan. In the middle of her lower wing was a gap.

'That's where I'll be lying,' said the Colonel. 'Across here.'

'You lie down?' frowned Taddy. 'To fly?'

'That's right,' said the Colonel, 'less wind resistance. And I got wires, right by my hand. So I can work the tail, steer her where I want her to go.'

Taddy said, 'By thunder! I reckon Hawk is the bestest flying machine in the land!'

The Colonel smiled, patted Taddy's

shoulder. 'I couldn't have put it better myself, partner.'

Taddy beamed. He squirmed with pride and pleasure – he just couldn't help himself.

Then the Colonel added, 'But she'd better be good. There's plenty of fellers tried it before me and failed.'

'Where are they now ?' asked Taddy. Were they in barns somewhere, making other flying machines that might beat Hawk to the prize?

'Mostly they're six feet under, son. Some with every bone in their body broken.'

At first, Taddy didn't understand. 'You mean, they got killed?'

The Colonel didn't reply. All he said was, 'Conquering the skies ain't no tea party.'

Taddy was shocked. *What if the Colonel died?* It made him shudder just to think about it.

But then Taddy reminded himself, he survived a bear attack! He had the scar on his neck to prove it. He'd been chased by Sioux braves, swum raging torrents. A man like the Colonel wasn't easy to kill.

Besides, he couldn't die. Taddy just couldn't imagine it. The Colonel was so bursting with life, like a glorious sunrise. He made everyone else look grey and boring.

Beside him, decided Taddy, all the other folks I know is as boring as – as cow muck.

'We'll take her out on her first flight,' said the Colonel. 'Just got to wait for the glue to dry.'

He paced restlessly round the barn.

'We'll be ready, kid,' he told Taddy, his blue eyes shining. 'We can do it. You betcha!' He punched the air with his fist.

Taddy believed him. Like he believed everything the Colonel said.

'You betcha!' he echoed, punching the air too.

While they waited, Taddy dared to ask something.

'You know when you said you was a sharpshooter. Could you hit that nail up there?'

Taddy pointed to a nail, sticking out of a rafter, high up in the roof of the barn.

The Colonel stopped pacing. He squinted up at it. 'Well,' he drawled, 'I ain't got my trusty silver Colt with me. But I could hit that for sure. I could hit a fly in the eye at fifty paces!'

'Will you teach me one day, to do that?'

'Sure thing,' promised the Colonel.

Taddy was thrilled. He thought he'd be a crow-scarer forever. He couldn't see any other future. Now he was building flying machines, soon he'd learn to be a sharpshooter. Life, that had seemed so dreary before, was suddenly full of rainbows.

'We need some help,' said the Colonel suddenly, 'to launch Hawk.'

'Do we?' Taddy tried not to show his dismay. 'I thought it was a secret,' he said, jealously. 'Just between you and me.'

The Colonel laughed. 'It won't be a secret once this little beauty's airborne. Folks will see her for miles around. They'll think it's a miracle. An angel maybe, sent from Heaven! Folks still don't believe that men can fly. But we know different, don't we Taddy?'

Taddy laughed, along with the Colonel. He could just imagine how they'd point, how their eyes'd pop.

He pictured the old devil, his red face turned upwards, his mouth open like a baby bird's.

He'll think it's a giant eagle, thought Taddy. Come to gobble his seed!

Then, through the open barn door, Taddy heard a faint sound, *Clack, clack, clack, clack.*

William!

'I know someone to help,' he told the Colonel.

His jealous feelings vanished. He didn't mind sharing the Colonel and Hawk with William.

He raced to the Top Field. 'William. You're needed!'

William was standing like a scarecrow in the middle of the field. What was he thinking? Who could tell. He turned slowly round, his face one big question mark. 'But Master told me to stay put,' he said.

'The Colonel's more important than Master,' said Taddy, tugging William's tatty sleeve. 'Master ain't fit to clean the Colonel's boots.'

'But Master said,' insisted William, 'don't you dare move, boy. Not unless them clouds fall down.' William stared up at the high, white clouds racing overhead. 'And they ain't fallen down yet.'

'The old devil was making fun of you,' said Taddy, dragging him off. 'Besides, Master won't say nothing. The Colonel's got him scared to death!'

Taddy shoved William in through the barn

door. William shambled over to the Colonel.

'Welcome son!' boomed the Colonel, holding out his hand.

'Shake hands with the Colonel,' said Taddy, giving William a nudge.

William stood, tongue-tied. He looked down at the floor. He shuffled his big boots. The Colonel let his hand drop.

'He's shy with strangers,' explained Taddy. 'We don't get many strangers round here. But he's strong. And he does what he's told. Long as you tell him in simple words.'

'He'll do just fine,' said the Colonel. 'Come on now, boys. Jump to it! We got no time to waste!'

CHAPTER FOUR

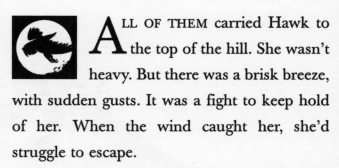 ALL OF THEM carried Hawk to the top of the hill. She wasn't heavy. But there was a brisk breeze, with sudden gusts. It was a fight to keep hold of her. When the wind caught her, she'd struggle to escape.

'See, boys, she's trying to fly already!' shouted the Colonel.

The tight silk on her wings twanged like the strings of a guitar.

Taddy's throat was dry. There was a

fluttering feeling inside him. It had begun when the Colonel had said, 'Time for her first flight.' The fluttering was getting worse. Soon it would be wild, beating wings.

He glanced up at William. William's face looked perfectly calm. He hadn't even seemed surprised when he'd seen Hawk. As if he saw flying machines every day of his life.

Ain't he excited? thought Taddy. Don't he know this is an *historic occasion*? It was impossible to tell.

'This is the spot,' said the Colonel, stopping and staring out at the view. Green fields stretched to the horizon. From up here, the sheep looked like tiny white fluff balls.

'Watch out, William!' cried Taddy. The wind tried to wrench Hawk out of their hands. William gripped the bamboo framework. But not too tightly. Hawk felt fragile to him, as if you could crush her like an egg.

'Whoa! She's bucking like a pony! Hold her down, boys!' cried the Colonel. The wind stung their faces, whipped their hair back.

'It's too blowy for my liking,' said the Colonel suddenly. 'But we ain't got time to be choosy.'

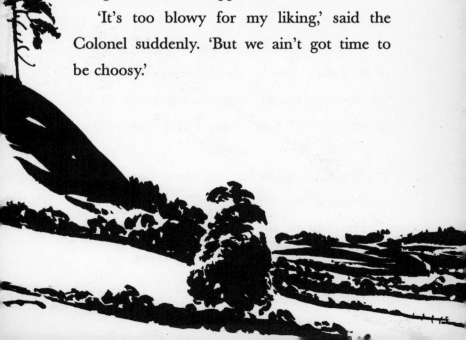

Taddy held one tip of Hawk's lower wing, William the other.

'Keep her steady,' said the Colonel, as he wriggled, belly down, on to the lower wing. 'Now run, boys, run!'

William and Taddy started running, to the edge of the hill.

Even with the Colonel on board, Hawk wasn't heavy. The wind took his weight.

Taddy thought, We're going to run off the hill top!

But then the Colonel cried, 'Let her go boys!'

Taddy let go. Flung himself to the ground, so he didn't tumble straight down the hill. He rolled over, stared upward, expecting to see Hawk soaring above him. There was nothing in the blue sky but clouds.

The Colonel cried, his voice hoarse with excitement, 'She's taking off!'

Hawk lifted, the wind got under her wings.

She reared up, like Starlight.

Then disaster. Her tail never left the ground. She crashed back to Earth, then slithered along the grass. Some bamboo poles snapped. The silk ripped. Halfway down the hill, she stopped.

'Colonel!' Taddy skidded down the hill, frantic with fear. What had the Colonel said about other aviators? 'Some are six feet under. Every bone in their body broken.'

'Colonel, are you hurt?'

A shaky voice came from among the bamboo poles and fluttering silk.

'I'm fine, boy. Just a few bruises.'

William came lumbering down the hill.

'The Colonel's safe!' Taddy told him. But Hawk was damaged. Her first flight over before it had even begun.

'*Darn,*' said the Colonel, scrambling out from between the wings. 'Hold her now, boy!' he warned William. 'Else the wind'll take her!'

He turned to Taddy. 'There just wasn't enough lift. She couldn't get off the ground!' His face was sick with disappointment.

'Does that mean she ain't never going to fly?' asked Taddy.

The Colonel stuck out his chin. Suddenly, his face was defiant. 'Don't never say never, boy!' he said to Taddy. 'You give up too easy. We got all day to make improvements. First, we take her back to the barn and patch her up.'

Taddy was ashamed of himself for doubting.

If anyone can make Hawk fly, he told himself firmly, Colonel Powhatten can.

William trudged back to crow-scaring. Before he went he told Taddy, smacking his lips, 'I got some bacon for me dinner!'

Taddy shook his head. How could William think about his dinner? When Hawk was going to fly, any minute?'

'I'll come and get you,' Taddy called after him, 'when we've mended Hawk.'

The Colonel was dragging Hawk down the hill, sliding her over the grass. Taddy hurried to help him. But suddenly, there was a big belly blocking his way, in corduroy breeches. Taddy looked up.

'Master!'

The farmer's face was red, But, for once, it wasn't scowling. It seemed almost merry.

'I was spying on you from behind the hedge,' said the farmer. 'Was he trying to make that heap of sticks fly? What a good joke! I nearly busted me britches!'

He stomped off, his belly still wobbling with laughter.

He looked back. 'If God had meant us to fly,' he said, 'he'd have given us wings.'

Taddy's hands clenched into fists. 'You old devil' he muttered under his breath. 'You don't know nothing! She'll fly. Just you wait and see!'

But there was fear behind his defiance. Would Master share his joke with the whole village? Hawk was supposed to be a secret, until tomorrow.

In the barn, Colonel Powhatten and Taddy stared at Hawk. They'd soon patched her up – the flying machine was as good as new. But that wasn't the main problem.

'She just didn't have enough lift,' said the Colonel. Starlight nuzzled his neck. Absent-mindedly, he reached out to stroke her nose. 'She was trying to take off. But she couldn't.'

Taddy scrunched up his face, to show the Colonel he was thinking hard too. But his brain felt like a big black hole.

Then, suddenly, his head filled with birds. He saw a barn owl, out hunting, skimming the ground. He saw swifts, skittering about high in the sky.

Taddy punched the air in excitement. 'I got the answer! I've studied birds – ain't you ever seen swifts, Colonel? They don't land on the ground. 'Cos if they do they can't take off 'cos their wings is too thin to lift them and –'

Taddy stopped, the Colonel looked mystified. You ain't explaining right! Taddy scolded himself. He tried again. He spoke more slowly this time.

'Have you seen barn owls then? They got really short, wide wings.' Taddy stretched out his arms, pretending to be an owl. 'And they don't even have to flap 'em. Those wings just lift 'em up, let 'em float –'

The Colonel interrupted, just as excited as Taddy. 'Why did I follow those useless plans? I should have used my own brains –'

'But I thought you drew them plans yourself?' Taddy butted in.

'Never mind about that now, boy,' said the Colonel briskly. 'You're saying Hawk needs wide, short wings? Same as an owl? Then she'll lift off the ground?'

Taddy nodded eagerly.

'By thunder, boy, I think you're right! Let's

jump to it. Get me a bale of silk! And some of them bamboo poles!'

It was late afternoon. Taddy and the Colonel sat slumped on the barn floor.

'I am dog-tired,' said the Colonel. 'But that sure was a smart idea you had, son.'

Taddy beamed. He was exhausted. His clothes were sticky with glue, his hair clogged with sawdust. But all he cared about was Hawk. Her long, slender wings were gone. He and the Colonel had made her brand-new ones, shorter and twice as wide.

'I reckon she'll lift off now,' said the Colonel. He dragged a weary hand over his face. 'Mind if I make a confession, partner?'

Taddy looked at him, mystified.

But the Colonel carried on, as if it didn't matter if anyone was listening. He seemed to be talking to himself.

'When I first got interested in this flying

thing, it was on account of the prize money. I thought, I sure could use that five hundred pounds. But now, I don't care two hoots about that. It wouldn't even matter if there was no money at the end of it.' The Colonel stopped, shook his head, as if he was amazed by his own foolishness. Then he shrugged, as if it couldn't be helped.

'Fact is, all I want is to see her fly.'

The Colonel's last words made perfect sense to Taddy. 'That's what I want too, more than anything!' He was already scrambling to his feet. 'I'll go and get William.' He couldn't wait to give Hawk another test flight.

He dashed outside. 'Hey, Taddy! Wait!' someone called to him. Taddy spun round. A heavy horse was clopping along the farm track. A boy rode it, bareback. Taddy knew him. His ma owned the inn, in the village.

'That Colonel feller in the barn?' he asked Taddy.

Taddy scowled up at the boy.

He wanted the Colonel all to himself. He hated having to share him. 'What you want him for?' he asked suspiciously.

'None of your business,' said the boy, riding right into the barn. Taddy could hear Starlight whinnying a welcome to the cart horse.

Taddy didn't run to fetch William. Instead, he slid into the barn and stood in the shadows, listening.

'What's that there box of tricks?' the boy asked the Colonel rudely, pointing at Hawk.

Taddy drew in a sharp breath. He almost said out loud, 'You're talking to a Wild West hero! Where's your manners?'

But the boy wasn't overawed by the Colonel. He didn't seem to think the Colonel was god-like.

'There's some fellers from London, waiting for you back at the inn,' said the boy.

Could Taddy even hear scorn in the boy's

voice as he spoke to his hero? No, it wasn't possible!

'You're to come back straightaway,' said the boy.

To Taddy's amazement, the Colonel did as he was told. He picked up his jacket.

Taddy couldn't keep quiet any longer. He sprang forward. 'You're not going, are you?'

The Colonel saw Taddy's desperate disappointment. He hesitated, appeared to change his mind. 'Well, maybe I could –' he started to tell Taddy.

But the boy from the inn butted in. 'Them men from London said, "If this Colonel geezer don't turn up soon, we're off".'

'I'm on my way,' said the Colonel, fitting on his white hat.

'But we need to try out Hawk's new wings!' said Taddy. 'You can't just leave!'

The Colonel looked flustered. He leaned down to whisper in Taddy's ear. 'I can't afford not to. We need that reporter and photographer. They're witnesses. They'll tell the world about Hawk. Without them, even if she wins the prize, who's going to believe it?'

'But I want us to fly her now!' said Taddy. 'Just us two.'

'Tomorrow,' said the Colonel, leading Starlight out of the barn. 'Tomorrow's the big day. You'll see her fly, I promise. Go home for a bite to eat. Then come back here and stand guard. I don't want nothing to happen to Hawk tonight. Will you do that for me, son?'

He fixed Taddy with his electric blue eyes.

Taddy nodded. Of course he would do that. He would do anything the Colonel asked.

The Colonel went trotting off on Starlight. Then seemed to remember something. He turned round, swept his white hat three times around his head, reared Starlight up. 'See you, partner!'

Then he urged Starlight into a gallop.

'See you, partner,' echoed Taddy. But the Colonel was already gone.

'Partner!' sniggered the boy from the inn as he clomped off, on his big, clumsy horse. 'Ain't you forgetting, Taddy, you're just a raggedy crow-scarer?'

CHAPTER FIVE

TADDY WENT RACING home. He shouted, 'Ma!' She didn't answer. She was probably down the garden feeding the hens.

He snatched some bread and cheese and began running back to guard Hawk. He mustn't let the Colonel down.

But he met Meg, trailing along the lane.

'Shouldn't you be at work?' asked Taddy.

'They don't want me up at the Big House no more. I was cheeky to Cook,' Meg told him.

'Cook says, "That floor ain't scrubbed proper!" And me arms ached so bad! They was torture! And I'm so sick of being bossed about. So I says, "Do it yourself then, you old witch!"'

'That's bad,' said Taddy, frowning and shaking his head. 'But I got to go!'

'Then I throws the scrubbing brush at her,' said Meg. Taddy stared.

'You didn't! Ma'll kill you! She'll tan your hide!'

'I know,' said Meg, snivelling and wiping her snotty nose. 'That's why I durstn't go home.'

Taddy felt sorry for her. But he had no time for her troubles. The Colonel was counting on him. He started hurrying away. 'I can't stop! Tell Ma I'm sleeping at the barn tonight,' he shouted over his shoulder.

Then Meg said something that made him stop dead. 'Cook was talking about that Colonel again.'

Something inside Taddy warned him, Don't ask! But he was so curious, he just couldn't help it. He went walking back to Meg. 'What did she say?'

'She says she knows him.'

'What?' said Taddy. 'But he hasn't been up to the Big House. He'd have told me.'

'No, she knows him from years ago, from when they was children.'

'Is Cook American then?' asked Taddy. 'I never knew that!'

'No, noddle brain!' snapped Meg. She felt spiteful. She wanted to make someone else's day as bad as hers had been.

'Cook says, "He can *pretend* to be a fine gentleman. He don't fool me." She says, "He's no more American than I am!" She says, "Powhatten, my foot! His real name's Walter Claridge!"'

'I don't understand!'

'It's simple enough, ain't it?' said Meg.

'Cook says he grew up in her village. She says, "All them fancy clothes! I could laugh! He was a farmboy when I knew him. With clothes a beggar would have turned up his nose at!"'

'Farmboy?' said Taddy, as if he was in a trance. 'Walter Claridge? I don't believe it! I don't believe a single word! That stupid Cook made a mistake. Colonel Powhatten isn't Walter Claridge!'

'There's proof,' said Meg. 'Cook says he's got a scar on his neck. From falling out of a

tree when he was stealing apples. Has he got a scar on his neck?'

'No, he hasn't!'

'Cook says he was a cringing little thing. Always getting beaten by the farmer. But he told these big, boasting lies. Cook says, "We used to laugh fit to bust at Walter! He said things like –"'

'Shut up! Shut up!' screeched Taddy, clamping his hands over his ears.

'Like one day, I'll go far away, I'll be rich and famous!' finished Meg triumphantly.

Then Meg's look turned to gloom again. Her lip quivered, 'I bet I get a beating off Ma.' But Taddy wasn't listening. He still had his hands over his ears.

She shuffled off down the lane. She was barefoot. Her boots came with the job. When she was sacked, Lady Violet had taken them back.

Slowly, slowly, Taddy uncovered his ears. All he could hear was the mocking sound of crows cawing over his head.

'It's not true! It's not true!' he muttered furiously clenching his fists by his side.

Taddy pictured the Colonel, splendid on Starlight, rearing up, sweeping his hat round his head like a halo.

He saved you from the old devil, Taddy reminded himself.

I don't believe a single word that old witch says. She's an evil, wicked old woman. Spreading lies about the Colonel.

Taddy stomped back to the barn, muttering wild, bloodcurdling threats against the Cook. 'If she was a cockroach, I'd squash her flat!'

But in the barn, he calmed down. It was quiet and peaceful. Doves cooed in the rafters.

Taddy walked around the flying machine. She's beautiful, he thought. Like a glittering dragonfly that's settled for a second on the barn floor.

But she didn't whisk away, like dragonflies

always did. She was waiting for tomorrow, for her first proper flight. Them new wings will take her up, for certain, thought Taddy. He could already see her, high up in a blue sky, gliding with real hawks.

Who cares what Cook says? She don't matter. She's a cockroach. He pretended to squash her, stamping his bare foot on the ground so hard that it hurt.

Anyhow, tomorrow, when the Colonel flew Hawk and won the prize, no one would hear her wicked lies. The whole world, cheering and clapping the Colonel, would drown her out.

Taddy ate his supper. He curled up under Hawk's wing. Told himself, I'll just have a little rest.

With Hawk's wing sheltering him, he closed his eyes. He felt safe, protected.

Two minutes later, the sound of his gentle snoring filled the barn.

CHAPTER SIX

Taddy opened his eyes. He looked up, dazzled. There was a gauzy golden sheet above him. What was it? Then he realised – it was Hawk's wing, glittering in a shaft of sunlight. He'd overslept!

It's late! thought Taddy, leaping to his feet. You lazy layabout!

He hurried to the barn door, threw it wide open. Bright sunshine made him blink. A light breeze lifted his hair. It was a perfect day for flying.

Taddy could hardly wait. He was fizzing with excitement.

Today Colonel Powhatten would keep Hawk in the air for a whole minute and win the prize. The photographer from London would take his picture.

And the reporter'll tell the world! thought Taddy.

There was a trough of water outside the barn. It was green and scummy.

Better make myself smart. Taddy didn't want to let the Colonel down. He didn't want those important men from London to think, 'Who's this raggedy country urchin?'

He splashed water on his face, made his shaggy hair wet, tried to smooth it down.

It kept springing up into spikes. 'No!' he wailed to himself. 'Why does it do that?' He slapped it down, again, ferociously.

There was nothing at all he could do about

his shabby clothes, the holes in the knees of his trousers, his bare feet.

Don't matter, decided Taddy, giving up.

The newspaper men wouldn't be interested in him. They wouldn't take his picture. They would put headlines in the paper, 'COLONEL POWHATTEN CONQUERS THE SKIES!'

They won't write about me, thought Taddy. They won't say Hawk's new wings was my idea.

He didn't feel resentful. It was only right that the Colonel should have all the glory. He just felt honoured to be here.

At an historic occasion, Taddy told himself, proudly.

But where was the Colonel? Why wasn't he here? He'd said, 'I'll be there tomorrow, boy, bright and early!'

Taddy looked up to the hill top. It was empty. He looked down the track to the barn. It was empty too. He rushed to the corner. The lane to the village stretched away into the distance. He'd expected to see Starlight trotting up, with the Colonel waving his hat, 'Howdee, Partner! Ready for the big day?'

But there was no one coming this way. There wasn't a single living soul anywhere.

Taddy rushed back to the barn to wait. He didn't want to leave Hawk alone for long.

'He'll be here any minute!' he shouted into the barn. It didn't feel strange, talking to a flying machine. He already thought of Hawk as a living thing. She would be as impatient as he was. Itching to get up there, among the clouds.

But minutes passed. Then hours.

'*Caw! Caw!*' Crows wheeled over him. Their cries seemed to mock his hopes. 'Look, we can fly. It's so easy!'

Still Taddy wasn't disheartened. The sun rose higher and higher in the sky. It was getting sweltering hot. He picked a big, cabbagey leaf. Swished it over his head to keep off the flies that were buzzing round him.

Still no one came. There was an eerie silence everywhere. Even the crows were snoozing, in the midday heat.

Clack, clack, clack, clack. Taddy heard the clatter of the bird-scarer. William wasn't taking a rest. He must be in the Top Field. Taddy couldn't see him. But knowing William was nearby made him feel less lonely.

Every now and then, he rushed to the corner, his heart fluttering with hope.

And every time, his hope fizzled out.

Wait! There was a horse coming down the lane. He could hear its hooves.

'I knew he'd come!' Taddy's face lit up in a huge, delighted grin.

But it wasn't the Colonel. The boy from the inn came plodding round the corner on his big, heavy cart horse.

'Wotcha doing?' asked the boy.

'I'm waiting for the Colonel.' Taddy didn't like this boy. He had a sneery face and a voice to match. But he had to ask, 'Have you seen him?'

'Why, ain't you heard?' said the boy in his teasing voice. 'He's scarpered.'

'Scarpered?'

'In the night,' said the boy. 'Without paying his bills. Ma was hopping mad. They was on to him, you see.'

'Who was?' asked Taddy, bewildered.

'The poliss,' said the boy, licking his lips. He was thrilled to be the first to tell Taddy the bad news. Nothing this exciting had happened in the village for a long time. 'Three constables come sniffing round last night, asking for him. Soon as he saw 'em, he legged it. Out the window, on his hoss and away! You should have seen him ride!'

'But why?' said Taddy struggling to make sense of the boy's story. 'Why was they after him? He's a big hero.'

The boy from the inn gave a mocking laugh. 'A big liar, more like! "He often pretends to be an American Colonel. It fools simple folk." That's what the constables said. They said, he's a very clever trickster. That he cheated a *real* aviator out of them plans.'

Taddy exploded with anger. 'I don't believe you! He was a real aviator!'

'No, he weren't,' said the boy, smugly. 'No more than he was a real Colonel. He was just after that prize money. He weren't in Buffalo Bill's Wild West show neither. That was just more of his boasting. And he ain't never set foot in America,' added the boy.

'That's wicked lies!' shrieked Taddy, bursting out crying. 'He did! He wrestled with a grizzly bear!'

'Ha, ha. You believed all them stories, didn't you? You was really taken in! I knew he was a fake soon as I saw him –'

'I'll kill you!' screeched Taddy.

His face twisted with tears and fury, he hurled himself at the boy. Grabbed his leg, tried to drag him off the horse. He didn't know he had such strength or hatred in him. 'I'll kill you for what you just said about the Colonel!'

'Git off! Git off! I'll tell my ma of you!' The boy clung on to the horse's mane. 'You're a maniac, you are! You should be locked up!' He

kicked Taddy in the face, then dug his heels into the cart horse, 'Git on, yer big stupid lump!' The big horse plodded slowly off.

When he was at a safe distance, the boy turned round. His voice was shrill and scared. But he wanted his revenge.

'And that pile of sticks back there in the barn. Everyone's laughing 'emselves silly about that. You never thought it would fly, did you?'

At last, the boy's jeering voice faded away. Long after he'd gone, Taddy was still crouching, his face covered with his hands.

The things the boy had said about the Colonel whirled around in his head – *fake, liar, trickster, all he cared about was the prize money.*

'He didn't care about the money,' muttered Taddy. 'He didn't! All he wanted was to see Hawk fly!'

Other folk might laugh themselves silly. But Taddy still had faith. In his head a plan began to unfold, so wild and daring it made him shiver.

Someone called his name. Taddy didn't even hear.

'There you are!' said Meg, scrambling into the ditch beside him. 'You'll never guess! I didn't get a hiding last night. Ma says, "I was going to tell you to hand in your notice. I've got a better place in mind for you, my girl." Taddy, Taddy, I'm talking to you!' Meg shook his arm. No answer. She pulled his hands away from his face. Even now he didn't seem to notice her. His eyes were starry and faraway.

'*Ooo*, Taddy? What's wrong with your nose? It's all swelled up.' She prodded it.

'*Ow*,' said Taddy, forced out of his trance.

'Did you get in a fight?'

Taddy shook his head, as if that wasn't important. 'Listen Meg. I'm going to fly

Hawk,' he told her, his eyes burning with purpose. 'I'm going to show 'em all. But you got to help me. You and William.'

CHAPTER SEVEN

'GO AND FETCH William,' said TADDY.

Meg opened her mouth to say, You can't give me orders!

But Taddy was already on his way back to the barn.

Meg shouted, 'That Walter Claridge. He fooled everyone good and proper.'

'His name's not Walter Claridge,' said Taddy. 'It's Colonel Powhatten.'

Meg shook her head. 'No one believes that

any more but you, Taddy,' she whispered.

But Taddy wouldn't believe it. Couldn't believe it.

'The police made a mistake,' he muttered. 'That Cook is a wicked old witch! That boy at the inn, he's just jealous the Colonel chose me and not him!'

The Colonel had had to leave in a big hurry. But Taddy wouldn't let him down.

'I'm going to win that prize,' he told himself, 'I'm going to make Hawk fly.'

Hawk was waiting in the barn. Even here, when tiny gusts of wind sneaked in, her silky wings lifted. They rustled and shimmered. As if she couldn't wait to take off.

Taddy checked over his shoulder, to see if Meg and William were here. They would think he was mad, talking to a flying machine. But there was no sign of them yet.

'They're saying horrible, cruel things about Colonel Powhatten,' Taddy whispered to

Hawk. 'That he's not a Colonel. That he's not even a real aviator. That he only cared about the money. When you and me fly, we'll make 'em eat their words. We'll make 'em –'

Taddy suddenly stopped talking. Meg had come racing in. William came plodding after her. He still had his bird-scarer in his hand. He looked worried.

'Master says –' he began.

'I know!' said Taddy. 'You mustn't move unless the clouds fall down. Forget what Master said. This is important.'

Meg was worried too. 'Taddy, you'll get into such trouble –'

'I don't want to hear!' said Taddy, jamming his hands over his ears. When he took them away again, Meg was saying, 'You ain't allowed.'

'Yes, I am,' said Taddy. 'I helped make 'er! It's 'cos of me she's got them new wings.'

'But you don't know how to fly. Ain't it dangerous?'

Taddy didn't answer this question. Instead he said, 'Let's jump to it!'

He dashed towards Hawk. He didn't want to hear any more warnings. He was scared. But he'd decided to fly Hawk and no one was going to talk him out of it.

Then he skidded to a stop. He'd suddenly thought of something. He spun round. 'We need witnesses!' he said. 'It ain't no good without 'em! Those newspaper men, did they go back to London?'

Meg shook her head. 'I don't know, Taddy. Shall I run to the village and find out?'

Taddy thought, If they come, they might stop me. They'd just see a ragged, eleven year old crow-scarer. Not the partner of Colonel Powhatten. They might even chase him away. 'You don't belong here, boy!'

'Don't matter about them,' he said. 'You can be a witness, Meg. You can tell them all what happened.'

It was no use asking William. He wouldn't remember. He couldn't hardly remember how to put on his own trousers.

'Help me carry Hawk,' said Taddy. 'Hurry, hurry!'

It made him frantic to think that some grown-up might interfere, before he'd got Hawk off the ground. Once he was up there, it wouldn't matter. No one could reach him. They could shout and threaten all they liked. The old devil could shake his fist: 'Git back down here, boy!' He wouldn't hear them. It would just be him and Hawk, swooping together through the blue sky.

They staggered up the hill. Hawk was light as a kite. But the wind plucked at her wings, tried to snatch her from them. Little Meg hung on grimly. She might be tiny, but she had strong muscly arms from scrubbing floors at the Big House.

Taddy had terrible visions of Hawk

escaping, tearing out of their hands and taking off without him. 'Don't leave me behind!' he wanted to say.

On the hill top, William and Meg held Hawk steady. Taddy crawled aboard, lay stretched out flat on Hawk's lower wing.

Poles and silk creaked and twanged all around him. Hawk trembled, like a captive wild bird.

'Run!' shrieked Taddy. 'Don't forget to watch. You're a witness.'

They'd believe Meg. She was sensible. 'She's got her head screwed on right,' said Ma. 'She don't daydream *her* life away.'

'I got to stay in the air for one minute,' yelled Taddy. 'You got to time me!'

Then, 'Wait!' Meg cried.

'Don't try to stop me!' warned Taddy.

'No! No!' said Meg. 'I ain't got a watch!'

'Count!' shrieked Taddy. 'Count to sixty!'

Then William was running again, holding

Hawk's wing tip. And Meg had to run hard to keep up with him. The wind dragged Taddy's hair back, scraped his cheeks.

'Let her go!' he screamed. But Meg already had. She'd been pulled off her feet and was slithering down the hill, face down in the mud.

Hawk juddered, started to nose dive. Taddy saw grass sliding beneath him. But then the wind caught her. Those new wings worked beautifully. She swooped up.

'Look Meg!' bellowed William, pointing.

Taddy felt himself being lifted. Then floating. The wind cradled them like a big airy cushion. He forgot to steer. Forgot about everything. Only one thing mattered.

'I'm flying,' whispered Taddy. He had a blissful smile on his face.

For glorious seconds, they drifted. Hawk was silent now, the only sound the wind shushing over her wings. Taddy didn't look

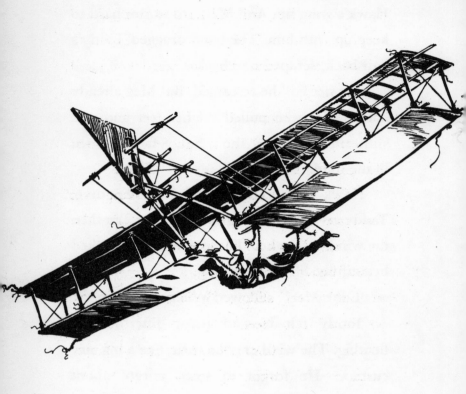

down. Only forward. All he could see ahead was blue. The thrill of it was almost too much to bear. 'I'm flying,' he whispered over and over again.

Then Hawk rocked.

'Eh?' Taddy grabbed a bamboo pole. There was another strong gust of wind. She tilted.

'Oh, no!' Taddy was hanging on desperately, his brain thrown into a panic. The wind flung Hawk about, like a plaything.

Far beneath him, Meg grabbed a tree root, stopped herself sliding. Bruised all over, she scrambled to her feet.

And saw Hawk plummeting to Earth, twisting and breaking up as she fell.

'Taddy!'

Taddy stopped seeing sky. He saw mud, rocks. They reared up at him. *Crunch* – Hawk hit the ground. Then he was tangled, trapped. He couldn't get free. He gave up, lay back and closed his eyes –

* * *

Meg reached him first. William was still on the hill top, pointing upwards. It hadn't reached his brain yet, that Hawk had crashed.

At first, Meg couldn't see Taddy in the wreckage. Hawk didn't look like a flying machine any more. Just a jumble of snapped poles and silk shreds.

'Taddy!' Meg threw some poles aside. There was Taddy, lying stretched out on his back.

He opened his eyes, gave her a wobbly smile.

'I thought you was dead!'

Taddy tried to move. 'Ow!' he screamed. 'I think I've broke me leg.'

'I'm going to get help,' said Meg. 'I'm going to get Ma!'

'Wait!' said Taddy. 'How long? How long was we in the air?'

It must have been more than a minute. It felt like forever.

Meg was already rushing away. Taddy

shouted after her. 'Did we win the prize?'

Meg didn't stop. But she shouted back over her shoulder. 'I don't know, Taddy. I fell over. I never counted! I never saw nothing!'

CHAPTER EIGHT

WILLIAM HELPED THEM lift Taddy out of the wreckage of the flying machine. They carried him gently back home on an old pig-sty door. He didn't open his eyes or speak the whole way. There was no knowing what was going on in his head.

Ma, who usually took charge, seemed thrown into a panic.

'Mercy me! What's the boy done to himself?'

It was Pa who knew what to do. 'Best fetch

the doctor,' he told Meg.

Meg went racing off to the village.

Ma burst out, 'I wish I could get my hands on that Colonel Powhatten, as he calls himself. He's the cause of all this trouble. It's him what made the boy believe he could fly!'

But Pa just said, 'We should get him into bed. William, will you help me lift him?'

William trudged back to work. On the way, he passed Hawk. She was just a broken skeleton of bamboo poles. The silk on her wings torn and fluttering like sad flags.

William sighed. She would never fly again. In his head he could still see her, soaring like a big, glittering bird. He'd never seen anything so beautiful in his whole life.

William twirled the rattle, *Clack, clack.*

'*Yaaa!*' He ran after the crows. But his heart wasn't in it. He felt a dreary sadness he couldn't explain. A scowling face appeared over the hedge.

'Put yer back into it boy!'

It was the old devil. Usually, he had more to say to his sheep dog than he did to William. But today, he seemed eager to stop and chat.

'I knew that Colonel Powhatten weren't no good. And now I been proved right. Pity that boy didn't have the brains to see it.'

'But –' stuttered William. He stopped, twisted his big hands together. He never spoke back to Master. But today he had something really important to say. He wanted to tell the world what he'd just seen.

'Taddy flew!' William burst out. He tried to find words to describe it. But somehow, they weren't in his head. So he flapped his arms instead.

'He flew!' he insisted again. He peered into Master's face to see if he understood. 'High up. He flew for a long time.'

'Flew?' said Master. William nodded violently. Nearly shook his head off.

'Flew?' said Master again. Then he started laughing. He doubled up, hugging his belly. He slapped his thighs. Puzzled, William waited for him to stop. What was Master finding so funny?

Master wiped his eyes, wheezed out a warning. 'Boy,' he said, 'you'd better not go spreading that around. Folks here already know you're an idiot. Do you want them to think you're a raving lunatic? They'll lock you away. They will!'

Later, on the farm, William met the cow man.

'What's this I hear, lad,' asked the cow man, 'about Taddy flying that machine? It can't be true, can it?' He was a kindly man. He knew William had more sense in his head than most people supposed.

William started to blurt out his story. But then, suddenly, he clamped his lips shut. He'd remembered what Master had said. He didn't want to be locked away.

'But wasn't you the only one to see it?'

asked the cow man. 'That must have been a fine sight!'

In his head, William could see it, as sharp as when it happened. Hawk, like a great sparkling kite, blue sky all around her. He ached to tell someone.

But then, *Shhh*! he told himself, sternly. He made his eyes dull and empty. He put a finger to his lips to seal them. He shook his head, swinging it from side to side like a bull.

'So you didn't see it then?' asked the cow man.

William didn't answer. He played dumb. And carried on, very slowly, shaking his head.

CHAPTER NINE

TADDY LIFTED UP his face to the sunshine. He was sitting outside in the garden with Pa, among the gooseberry bushes. It was very quiet and peaceful. His brothers were playing in a dirt heap down by the hens. Ma was working up at the Big House, doing the laundry. Meg was in her new place as a maid, for an old lady in the village.

Meg said, 'She's an old fusspot, but she's miles better than Cook. And I gets to eat until me belly is nearly bursting!'

Pa put down the piece of wood he was whittling. When he was well enough he carved things – toys for Taddy's little brothers. He usually carved farm carts and pull-along cows. But today, he'd done something different. He handed it, hesitantly, to Taddy.

'I know it ain't like the real thing,' he apologised.

'It's Hawk!' said Taddy. She looked clumsy, made out of wood. She wasn't airy and light. She looked earthbound, as if she could never take off. But Taddy was grateful. At least Pa had tried to understand. 'Thanks, Pa,' he said.

'How's your leg today?'

Taddy shrugged, 'Don't hurt much no more.'

His left leg was in wooden splints, wrapped round tight with bandages. He wriggled his grimy bare toes. The leg was getting better. He could even hobble around on it. Soon, he'd be able to go back to bird-scaring.

Pa frowned. Ever since the accident, Taddy had hardly spoken. Ma was getting sick of it. 'What's got into the boy?' she kept asking. 'He's no cause to mope about like this. He's lucky he wasn't killed.'

But Taddy didn't feel lucky. He'd lost Colonel Powhatten. He'd galloped away on Starlight, no one knew where.

Bet he's forgotten about me by now, thought Taddy.

He'd lost Hawk too. She'd been smashed to pieces. Without them both, there was a big empty hole in his life. He couldn't bear thinking about it – the time when he had wings. When he and Hawk rode the wind.

We conquered the skies! thought Taddy, punching the air like Colonel Powhatten.

It was a pity nobody knew about it but him.

He'd stopped trying to persuade people he'd won the prize. They either laughed themselves silly, or said, 'Prove it'. But the only witness was William.

And he's such a noddle, he can't remember nothing about it! thought Taddy. Whenever you asked him, he just looked stupid and shook his head.

Like the rest of the village, Ma couldn't stop talking about the Colonel. She'd said, 'All that fancy talk and fancy clothes! And he was just plain Walter Claridge underneath! No better than you, Taddy. A muck shoveller and bird-scarer, that's what he was!'

But Taddy had crammed his hands over his ears, and shouted, 'I'm not listening!'

The garden gate clashed. It was Ma, coming back from the Big House. She was carrying something – a parcel, tied up with brown paper and string.

'I met the carter in the lane,' she said. 'He brought this all the way from the railway station. It's for you, Taddy.'

'For me?' Taddy had never had a letter, let

alone a parcel, in his whole life.

Ma looked as if she didn't want to hand it over. But Pa said, 'Let the boy open it.'

First Taddy turned it over in his hands. 'Where's it come from?' He and Pa inspected it. There was no clue. Just Taddy's name and address and lots of strange-looking stamps.

Pa squinted at them, 'Ain't they American?' he said.

Taddy started to say, 'But I don't know no one in –'

Then, for the first time since the accident, hope started fizzing inside him, like tiny bubbles.

He fumbled with the knots, couldn't untie them. Pa slashed them through with his whittling knife. The paper fell open.

It was a pair of boots. But not ordinary boots.

They were riding boots, of soft white leather, with fancy stitching and silver spurs.

It was late at night. Everyone in the cottage

was asleep but Meg and Taddy. They were sitting with their toes in the warm ashes of the fire. Taddy had his new boots beside him. He carried them everywhere with him, to make sure his brothers didn't steal them.

'Do you think they're really from *him*?' asked Meg.

'Course,' said Taddy. 'He's gone back to America. I would too, if folk were telling such awful lies about me.'

'Have you tried them on yet?'

'I can't,' said Taddy. 'Not with me broken leg.'

'You could try one of them on.'

'All right then.'

Taddy brushed the ashes off his toes. He started tugging on the right boot. 'There's something in here,' he said. He took it off, plunged his hand inside.

Jammed in the toe of the boot was a screw of white paper. Taddy pulled it out, untwisted it. 'There's writing on it.'

He smoothed it out. Then handed it to Meg. 'Here. You can read better than me.'

Meg peered at the paper in the gloom. She followed the words with her finger. Her lips moved but no sound came out.

'What does it say?' begged Taddy. 'Hurry up, tell me!'

At last Meg said the words out loud.

'For Taddy,' she read. She stumbled over a word. Puzzled it out. Then read the whole message.

'For Taddy, Who'll Have His Own Wings One Day.'

CHAPTER TEN

'*Yaaa!*' YELLED TADDY. He rushed towards a crow, clacking his bird-scarer. '*Shoo!* You greedy seed-gobbler!'

His leg was mended now. It was a bit stiff. But he could still chase after crows.

The crow looked at him with its bright, mocking eye. Then rose lazily into the air and flapped away.

Time for me dinner, thought Taddy.

He wasn't scared to take a break for his

dinner. Or even to have a little rest. The old devil still lost his temper. But he didn't beat Taddy these days. Perhaps he thought that the Colonel might get to hear about it.

Taddy sat down and unwrapped his bread and cheese. The present from the Colonel, his precious riding boots, were beside him. He didn't dare wear them though. *Don't want to get them covered in cow muck.*

Ma had wanted to sell them. She'd said, 'I bet they cost a pretty penny. And they're far too good for you. They'll just get ruined in them muddy fields.'

Taddy had cried, 'No. They're mine!' and hugged the boots tightly to his chest.

Then to his surprise, Pa had stood up for him. Pa was feeling a lot stronger these days. His foot was healing up. The rags he wrapped around it weren't smelly anymore.

'No, let the boy keep them,' he'd said.

Ma had grumbled. In the end, though,

she'd nodded her head and agreed.

Then Pa had said, 'Suppose you don't want the carving of Hawk no more. Now you've got the riding boots from *him*.'

And Taddy had said, 'No, Pa! I want it. Honest I do. I'd never throw it away.' And Pa had looked pleased.

Taddy finished his bread and cheese. But he didn't go straight back to chasing crows. He had something important to do first.

He took some twigs off a bush, some thread and scraps of material out of his pocket. He began making tiny models.

William came trudging through the field.

'Watch out!' Taddy told him. He moved his models out of danger.

But William didn't crunch the models with his big boots. Instead he knelt down and poked his face right up to them.

'Flying machines!' he said.

'I been experimenting,' explained Taddy.

'Making wings all different sizes. Different shapes.'

'Do they fly?' asked William, amazed.

'Course they do,' said Taddy. 'That's the best one.'

William picked it up. Taddy almost said, 'Be careful!' William's big sausage fingers seemed about to crush it.

But William placed the flying machine very gently on his open palm. It trembled there, like a bright insect about to take off.

A puff of wind caught it. It was whisked into the air.

'It's flying!' said Taddy. Just watching it made him remember when he'd flown with Hawk. That thrilling feeling of freedom, of having the whole wide sky to swoop in.

William's face turned tragic. 'I can't see it no more. It's lost.' The tiny machine had whirled off into the blue.

'Don't matter,' said Taddy. 'I'll just make another one.' He was already biting off the thread with his teeth. This model would be better, fly even further.

'You should make a big one,' said William, suddenly. 'Like Hawk.'

Taddy looked up, surprised. He hadn't dared tell anyone his dreams. He was scared they'd laugh at him. But William seemed deadly serious. So Taddy blurted out, 'That's just what I'm going to do, William! I *thought* I was going to be a sharpshooter. But I don't

want to do that no more. I want to build my own flying machines!'

Still William didn't laugh. He nodded gravely, as if he approved. Then stumped away across the field.

Better get back to crow-scaring.

Taddy stashed his white boots under the hedge, so they wouldn't get wet if it rained.

Then he took a piece of paper out of his pocket. It was Colonel Powhatten's message. It had travelled across an ocean to reach him.

Taddy smoothed out the paper. Strangely, Colonel Powhatten was becoming a distant memory. He couldn't even remember what he looked like. But he knew the words of his message off by heart.

'For Taddy,' he murmured. 'Who'll Have His Own Wings One Day.'